CUTTING-EDGE CAREERS™

CAREERS IN
NANOTECHNOLOGY

Corona Brezina

ROSEN
PUBLISHING®
New York

Published in 2007 by The Rosen Publishing Group, Inc.
29 East 21st Street, New York, NY 10010

Library of Congress Cataloging-in-Publication Data

Brezina, Corona.
Careers in nanotechnology / Corona Brezina. — 1st ed.
    p. cm. — (Cutting-edge careers)
Includes bibliographical references and index.
ISBN-13: 978-1-4042-0955-8
ISBN-10: 1-4042-0955-7 (library binding)
1. Nanotechnology—Vocational guidance—Juvenile literature. I. Title.

T174.7.B73 2006
620'.5023—dc22

                                        2006023276

Manufactured in the United States of America

On the cover: Researcher with a scanning beam interference lithography (SBIL) machine.

CONTENTS

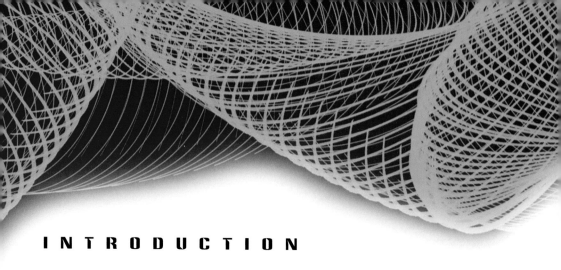

INTRODUCTION

[N]anotechnology is changing the world we live in, one small piece at a time. Indeed, nanotechnology works with very small pieces of matter. It involves research and development at the nanoscale level, particularly the range from 0.1 to 100 nanometers (nm). A nanometer is one-billionth of a meter. To put the size into perspective, a single strand of hair is about 75,000 nm in diameter, and the head of a pin is about a million nanometers across.

Foundations of a Nanotech Revolution

The concepts behind nanotechnology were first laid out by the Nobel Prize–winning physicist Richard Feynman in 1959, when he proposed that it was theoretically possible to engineer matter at the atomic scale. However, scientists were unable to explore the realm of the super-small until the 1980s, when new instruments allowed humans to view and manipulate atoms. It was around that time that scientists also discovered the first nanoparticles, molecules within the nanoscale range that are used for a variety of nanotech applications.

At the nanoscale level, matter begins to exhibit properties, or characteristics, different from those found at larger scales. A gold nanoparticle, for instance, has a different color and melting point

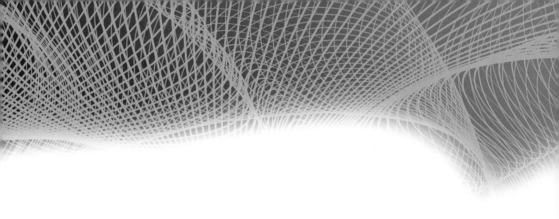

Richard Feynman is one of the most influential physicists in American history. He won the Nobel Prize in Physics in 1965 for his contributions to the field of quantum electrodynamics.

than a gold nugget. These novel properties can be exploited by incorporating nanoparticles into larger structures.

Researchers use either the "top-down" or the "bottom-up" method of fabricating structures at the nanoscale. In the top-down approach, a larger structure is precisely whittled away, leaving the desired product. In the bottom-up approach, individual atoms and molecules are put together piece by piece. This method often requires "self-assembly," where the components naturally assume the desired arrangement due to their size and shape, in addition to the laws of physics and chemistry. Both methods have advantages, although the top-down approach is easier to control.

President George W. Bush signs the 21st Century Nanotechnology Research and Development Act. In attendance was Richard Smalley, the Nobel Prize–winning nanotechnology pioneer *(3rd from left)*.

Government Support of Nanotechnology

On December 3, 2003, President George W. Bush signed the 21st Century Nanotechnology Research and Development Act. It authorized funding of $3.7 billion over a period of four years, the largest science initiative since the authorization of the space program. The act reaffirmed the National Nanotechnology Initiative (NNI) established during the administration of Bill Clinton.

On its official Web site (www.nano.gov), the NNI defines itself as "a federal R&D [research and development] program established to coordinate the multi-agency efforts in nanoscale science, engineering, and technology." In the near future, nanotechnology will become a major force in the world economy. The NNI aims to guarantee that the United States will remain at the cutting edge of nanotech development. It funds the creation of nanotechnology laboratories and supports research projects proposed by academic institutions, small businesses, and corporations. It encourages the development of a workforce skilled in nanotechnology that will be vital to industries transformed by nanotechnology, and it works to educate the public about the potentials of nanotechnology.

Tools of the Trade

The ultimate goal of most research and development projects is the creation of viable nanotech products. Whether this is accomplished by government labs, academic institutions, or private companies, the next step is manufacturing and marketing. Only one requirement remains for the foundations of a nanotech revolution: equipment capable of working with nanoscale materials.

The most important nanotech tools being used today are a class of instruments called scanning probe microscopes (SPMs). In addition to imaging, SPMs can be used to manipulate individual atoms. These instruments, and many other types of equipment used in nanotechnology, cost hundreds of thousands or even millions of dollars. As more companies and institutions establish nanotech programs, they will first require the tools for their research and development. Nanotechnology equipment manufacturing is a thriving industry with possible career potential. In the near future, nanotech labs and companies will continue to buy more equipment. There will be a market for improved instruments, specialized equipment, and basic inexpensive models. It is even possible that engineers will invent new instruments that will revolutionize the field of nanotechnology.

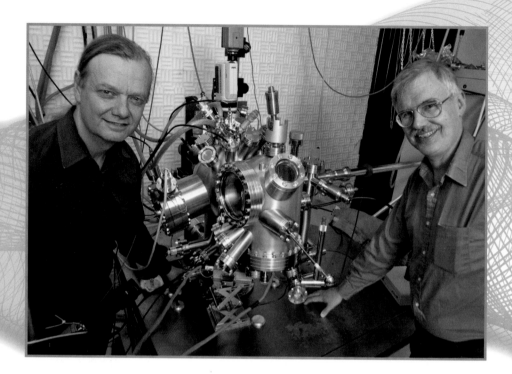

The first scanning probe microscope was constructed in 1981. It helped enable the early breakthroughs in nanotechnology.

A Promising Future

Any tennis fanatic has probably heard how nanotechnology has been used to improve the tennis rackets made by several manufacturers. To a novice, though, a tennis racket incorporating particles called nanotubes looks no different from any other. The effect of nanotechnology is demonstrated through the product's improved features, not by a flashy appearance. In this sense, the nanotechnology revolution will be an invisible one.

Many industries have a strong interest in nanotechnology. Nanomaterials have been incorporated into sports equipment, cosmetics, and clothing. Nanotechnology could bring about revolutions in health care and computing, and has potential in the energy and telecommunications industries. Concerns have been raised about possible environmental risks posed by nanomaterials, but when properly used, they could actually be used in environmental cleanup.

If nanotechnology is such a widespread phenomenon, you may wonder, why are there no nanotechnology stores in the mall? Where do you start looking for an entry-level job in such a promising field?

While nanotechnology will eventually transform many industries and affect our daily lives, it is still on the verge of making major commercial breakthroughs. Massive government grants, along with private investments, have led to the establishment of numerous labs and institutes across the country. Nanotechnology research and development is yielding promising results for future nanotech products, and many nanotech products are already on the market.

Nanotechnology currently requires a highly skilled and educated workforce. The number of nanotechnology jobs worldwide is expected to soar over the next decade. In the near future, there will be an exciting range of career paths open to nanotechnology-savvy professionals prepared to take advantage of the opportunities created by the expansion of the nanotech market.

CHAPTER 1

Preparing for a Nanotechnology Career

The field of nanotechnology ranges from pure scientific study to research and development to practical applications in a wide variety of fields. Regardless of the specific area of interest, a career in nanotechnology requires a solid background in science and technology. Today, most specialists in nanotechnology have advanced degrees in disciplines related to nanotechnology.

Going to School

Nanotechnology is such a new field that today's students will be the first generation to grow up in a world being changed by its applications. You can prepare yourself for a career in

John Zhou, winner of the International BioGENEius Challenge for high school students, is shown in a chemistry lab. His entry was a pathogen-detecting biosensor that used polymers as nanowires.

nanotechnology early on by signing up for advanced high school classes in chemistry, physics, biology, math, and computer science. Choose topics related to nanotechnology when you work on science fair projects, research papers, current events reports, and other independent assignments.

Extracurricular activities can also be a great opportunity to get involved in science- and technology-related organizations. Check out clubs, field trips, and competitions offered by your school or community. Many universities with nanotechnology programs also have tours, lectures, seminars, and summer programs for high school students and the general public.

When applying to colleges, do some thorough research on their nanotech programs. Do they specialize in a particular area of interest to you, like biological nanotechnology or nanoscale applications of information technology? Another option is to choose a broader major, like chemistry or computer science, and pursue nanotechnology at the graduate level. Graduate students can often earn recognition for research work even before earning a degree and gain hands-on work experience through internships.

Academic Centers of Nanotechnology

Along with providing funding for nanotech programs, the government is promoting the development of a workforce educated in nanotechnology to take on future nanotech jobs. Accordingly, the National Nanotechnology Initiative (NNI) has helped spur the establishment of nanotechnology centers in a number of universities across the country. The U.S. government has highlighted a handful of these programs, giving them the designation "Centers of Excellence in Nanotechnology."

Many of the best academic nanotechnology centers are located in or near hot spots for the nanotech industry. The University of California

James A. Cooper Jr., codirector of Purdue University's Birck Nanotechnology Center, poses in one of the building's labs. The heart of the facility is a 25,000-square-foot (2,323 square meters) nanofabrication clean room.

has established nanotechnology centers on several of its campuses, including Berkeley, Los Angeles, and Santa Barbara. In Massachusetts, Harvard University has brought together dozens of faculty members in creating its Center for Nanoscale Systems, in addition to other nanotechnology-related programs. The Massachusetts Institute of Technology (MIT) also has several nanotechnology programs. New York State has committed more than a billion dollars to nano-technology research and development. This has benefited Cornell University, Columbia University, and Rensselaer Polytechnic Institute, which boast some of the most prominent nanotechnology programs in the country. All three of these New York schools have been designated as Centers of Excellence by the federal government. In Texas, Rice University has distinguished itself as a research leader in nanotechnology, and it has established the Richard E. Smalley Institute for Nanoscale Science and Technology and the Center for Biological and Environmental Nanotechnology. A number of nanotech companies—including Zyvex, one of the most successful nanotech start-ups—are based in Texas around Dallas, Austin, and Houston. In the Midwest, Northwestern University has established the Center for Integrated Nanopatterning and Detection Technologies.

In most of these schools, the organization of the nanotechnology centers reflects the interdisciplinary nature of the field. Harvard's faculty for its Center for Nanoscale Systems is drawn from ten departments, including physics, engineering and applied sciences, chemistry and chemical biology, Harvard Medical School, and others. The members of Rice University's faculty that are affiliated with its Institute for Nanoscale Science and Technology include professors of anthropology, philosophy, economics, and religion, as well as the sciences, engineering, and mathematics.

Launching a Nanotech Career

Nanotechnology is full of potential applications that make it an exciting field for various government departments and private corporations. Some products on the market are already incorporating nanotech materials and processes. It is projected that the nanotech industry will soon be a major force in the economy. According to Lux Research, a firm specializing in nanotechnology research, nanotechnology will be a $2.6 trillion market worldwide by 2014.

The outlook is bright for future nanotech careers. According to the National Science Foundation, about 20,000 workers were involved in the nanotech industry worldwide in 2005. It expects that number to soar to two million over the next fifteen years. As the need for skilled nanotech workers increases, industries will actively recruit highly qualified candidates. Nanotechnology jobs will probably become less specialized, and more lower-level technical positions will open up as nanotechnology products gain a broader market.

Landing a Job

A student graduating from a university with a highly regarded nanotechnology program has an instant advantage: many universities have ties to private corporations and government programs. A university's career services department or a recommendation from a professor can be a great benefit in landing an interview for an attractive job. Job seekers can also check out technology job fairs and job listings in publications dealing with their field of interest. The Internet is another valuable tool, since job seekers can check out the Web pages of potential employers—many of them major companies—and look for job opportunities on online career centers.

It is not always obvious that the jobs advertised are related to nanotechnology. Here are a few sample job titles for positions that call for nanotechnology expertise:

Applications Engineer

Patent Agent

Research Scientist

R&D Chemist

Scientist, Drug Formulation & Encapsulation

Bill Conley, a graduate student at Purdue University's Birck Nanotechnology Center, demonstrates a computer model he designed to study friction at the atomic level.

Microfabrication Expert Technician

Biomedical Micro/Nanosystems Scientist

A close reading of the skills and requirements for the position will indicate what sort of nanotechnology background is necessary. It is always a good idea to do some background research on a potential employer, too. This will yield more information on the company's specific focus.

Established corporations such as IBM, Hewlett-Packard, Intel, DuPont, General Electric, Dow Chemical, Merck, ExxonMobil,

ChevronTexaco, and General Motors have an advantage in the resources they bring to nanotechnology research and development. They can afford to fund nanotechnology projects that will not yield an immediate profit. Most large corporations adopt a balanced strategy toward utilizing nanotechnology in their industries. In the short term, they use nanotechnology to improve existing products. In the long term, they pursue research and development that will enable them to remain innovative and competitive, and will perhaps transform their industries in the years to come.

Large corporations treat nanotechnology as a sideline, however, concentrating on the areas relevant to their industry. Many smaller businesses, such as Cambrios Technologies and Nanoplex, focus exclusively on cutting-edge nanotechnology. These companies, the pioneers of the nanotechnology industry, often pursue radically new and innovative paths of research and development. Not all of these businesses will succeed. Nanotechnology is a competitive industry, and a number of companies are racing to make breakthroughs in similar product areas, like solar cells, drug delivery systems, computer chips, and batteries. Smaller businesses, especially start-ups, are more likely to suffer from poor management or lack of financing. Still, the future of the nanotechnology industry holds great promise for smaller companies. It is likely that at least one or two will achieve a significant breakthrough in the field, just as Google emerged to become an Internet giant.

On the Sidelines

A graduate with a degree in nanotechnology will have a broad range of possible career choices: continuing in academia, taking a job in a government department, or choosing one of a variety of industries in which nanotechnology holds promise. But there is also a need for people knowledgeable in nanotechnology outside the hands-on career paths in the field.

A technician works at a lithography machine in the clean room of a nanofabrication lab at the New Jersey Nanotechnology Center.

In upcoming years, the business aspect of nanotechnology will become increasingly important. Some nanotech companies will see their value soar, while others will fail. There has already been discussion of a potential "nanotech bubble" sometime in the future, just as there was a "dot-com bubble" in the 1990s that led to a crash for Internet investors.

Many companies are founded by scientists, who may possess brilliant scientific credentials but no experience or talent for running a business. When nanotechnology starts to make a more significant impact on the economy, there will be ample opportunities for executives with a firm grasp of what is possible.

The emergence of nanotechnology also opens up niches elsewhere. Journalists and other science writers provide a window into nanotechnology for the public. Lawyers are already involved due to disputes over patent rights. As nanotechnology gains ground in the global economy, such cases will require expertise in international law.

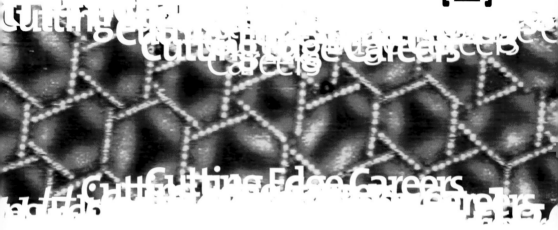

CHAPTER 2

Cutting Edge Careers
Cutting Edge Careers
Careers
Cutting Edge Careers

Everyday Nanotechnology

Nanotechnology is already creeping into our daily lives. Although the nanotech revolution is still in its infancy, industries have been quick to take advantage of the strength and other unique properties of nanotech materials. Various types of nanoparticles have been incorporated into cosmetics, clothing fibers, sports equipment, glass, and other commercially available products. Nanotechnology also has the potential to make computers more powerful and speed up telecommunications networks.

Producing Nanoparticles

Research, development, and production in the areas related to nanotechnology require premanufactured nanoparticles

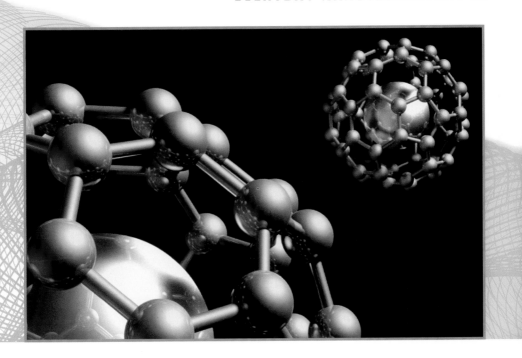

Above is a graphic of two buckyballs enclosing potassium ions. The carbon atoms that make up a buckyball connect to each other to form twelve pentagons and twenty hexagons on the molecule's surface.

and other basic nanomaterials. One of the first nanoparticles created was the buckminsterfullerene, often shortened to "buckyball" or "fullerene." Buckyballs are spherical molecules made up of sixty carbon atoms, measuring about one nanometer in diameter. Another nanoparticle, the carbon nanotube, consists of a lattice of carbon atoms forming a cylinder. It is useful for its light weight combined with a tensile strength greater than that of steel. Both of these carbon nanoparticles are used in the commercial manufacturing of various products. Yet another versatile nanoparticle is the quantum dot, or "nanocrystal." Because of properties resulting from the arrangement of its electrons, a quantum dot produces light when charged with energy. The specific wavelength of light emitted depends on its size and composition.

These silver nanowires lying on top of a calcium fluoride crystal were assembled from clusters of several thousand silver atoms using an atomic force microscope (AFM).

Supply companies manufacture these nanoparticles, as well as other nanomaterials such as nanowire, nanoclay, nanopowders, and nanocoatings. The market for nanomaterials will grow in coming years as more nanotech products are developed. It is a competitive market, and as a result, the high price of nanomaterials is already falling.

Nanomaterials manufacturing offers career opportunities in research and development, as well as production. To remain competitive in the future, companies will focus on developing high-quality and specialized products. Many companies already produce nanomaterials intended for specific applications in semiconductors, fuel cells, catalytic converters, flat-panel displays, plastics, health care, and various other industries.

On the Market

If there were a department store devoted exclusively to nanotech products, it would sell an astonishingly eclectic range of goods. From Tommy Hilfiger to 3M, companies are taking advantage of nanotechnology products and processes.

In the clothing department, you would find stain-resistant jeans, footwarmers for boots, and jackets studded with nanoparticles to reduce static cling. The sporting goods department would be quite extensive, featuring golf balls and clubs, baseball bats, tennis rackets, and soccer balls. The cosmetics department would offer a wide range of choices, such as sunscreens, makeup, and skin creams, including Fullerene C-60 face cream, which incorporates buckyballs. (L'Oréal, a cosmetics company, holds the third-highest number of nanotechnology-related patents of any company.) In the building materials department, you could find dirt-resistant glass and extra-durable paint. The automotive section would include tires made of improved rubber and components of car models, like the exterior panel of the Chevy Impala. There would even be a section for foods, containing items such as healthier canola oil. The jewelry department would display man-made diamonds, which also have great potential in industrial applications. This is only a small sampling of products that stem from nanotechnology.

Progress in this field has not yet revolutionized any industries or markets. Most commercial nanotech-based goods are improved versions of existing products. Regardless of whether a nanotech revolution does transform any industries, this trend will continue. In the interest of remaining competitive, companies will take advantage of improvements made possible by nanotechnology. In the coming years, we will see more and more familiar products enhanced by this branch of science.

This prospect for the future suggests excellent career opportunities for those interested in expanding hands-on applications of nanotechnology. Chemists, engineers, materials scientists, and other workers will be in high demand for their scientific expertise. The applications of nanotechnology materials and processes will cross over into many areas, from nutrition to the construction industry.

Computing and Telecommunications

In early 2006, *Forbes* magazine released its list of the top ten nano-tech products of 2005. Most of the entries reflected the current trend of using nanotechnology to improve existing products. At the top of the list, though, was Apple Computer's iPod nano, the pocket-sized MP3 player.

Is the iPod nano truly a nanotech device? Or is the "nano" descriptor just a marketing gimmick reflecting its small size? The chips in the iPod nano are indeed manufactured with nanoscale precision, an example of miniaturization taken to the molecular level. Samsung, the manufacturer of one of the iPod nano chips, achieves this using conventional chip fabrication techniques. In the near future, new techniques in chip fabrication will produce even smaller and more powerful chips. Nanotechnology holds great potential for future generations of products in industries such as computing, telecommunications, and electronics—industries that stay competitive by putting out smaller, faster devices.

The Next Computer Chip

Since the early days of computer technology, the electronics industry has been in a race to produce smaller, faster, and more powerful processors. Today, the basic building block of a computer chip is the transistor. Through a technique called photolithography, millions of transistors are etched onto a silicon wafer. The resulting interconnected assembly of components is called an integrated circuit.

Apple CEO Steve Jobs introduces the iPod nano in September 2005. The device's capabilities are made possible in part by nanoscale precision fabrication. However, many industry experts say that it is not a true nanotech device.

Faster processors are fabricated by shrinking transistors and cramming more transistors onto each chip.

The components of a computer chip are so small that they belong to a field called microelectronics. It would seem that the next step in miniaturization would be nanoelectronics. But microelectronic processes cannot be easily translated into the nanoscale. Photolithography at a nanoscale level is difficult and prohibitively expensive. Also, there is no certainty that nanoscale versions of today's transistors would function properly.

Nevertheless, the electronics industry is investigating innovative means of using nanotechnology in fabricating computer chips. In photolithography, the silicon chip is exposed to ultraviolet (UV) light. Nanotechnology offers various alternatives to photolithography, like electron-beam lithography, X-ray lithography, ion-beam lithography, and soft lithography, an easy method of reproducing patterns.

Another possible innovation involves completely replacing the silicon chip with new materials. A chip would consist of carbon nanotube transistors, nanowires, and organic molecules. A particularly radical approach to chip fabrication is the application of the bottom-up method of manufacturing. Instead of carving the circuit out of a chip, the structure would be assembled piece by piece from atoms and molecules.

Speeding Up Information with Nanotechnology

In addition to chips, nanotechnology holds potential in other areas of computing. Random-access memory (RAM) enables a computer, cell phone, or other device to access any piece of data in its storage system. Today, the dominant technology is dynamic RAM (DRAM). DRAM's main failing is that it requires a constant electrical current, therefore consuming a large amount of energy. A number of companies are investigating alternatives to DRAM, such as magnetic RAM (MRAM). MRAM uses properties of magnetic polarity, rather than a continuous electric current, to read data. It uses less energy and is faster than DRAM.

Nanotechnology may also hold the future of data storage. One of the most exciting products in development is IBM's Millipede device—named for its appearance—which records huge amount of nanoscale data onto a polymer plate. Not only does Millipede have an enormous capacity, it's also fast, energy-efficient, and inexpensive to fabricate.

Advances in display technology, from computer screens and cell phones to medical monitors, could impact telecommunications and the computing industry. The incorporation of nanotubes into a color screen can make it lighter in weight and more energy-efficient.

Behind the scenes, telecommunications and information technology could be revolutionized by new means of transmitting information. Today, long-distance phone calls and Internet data travel along fiber-optic networks, passing through slower electronic switches and routers along the way. An all-optical network that dispensed with such bottlenecks would drastically accelerate the speed of information. Nanotechnology has the potential to make that possible. Research has shown that buckyballs, for example, could be used in the creation of optical switches to replace the slower electronic versions.

Career Paths

Nanotechnology holds great promise for computing, telecommunications, and electronics, but for the most part, this promise has not reached the marketplace. Still, these industries offer excellent career opportunities for computer scientists, engineers, and hard scientists specializing in nanotechnology. In the near future, nanotech research and development will begin to yield actual products. Once these products have proved their effectiveness, companies will begin to focus on advancing their capabilities.

CHAPTER 3

Cutting Edge Careers

Nanotechnology's Prescription for Health Care

Our hypothetical department store of nanotech products would also have a small section devoted to health care. Wound dressing for burn victims incorporates nanosilver as an antibacterial agent. Abraxane, a nanoparticle breast cancer treatment drug, has been approved by the Food and Drug Administration (FDA). Nanotech materials are being used in dentistry as adhesives and tooth fillings.

Health care is one of the areas where nanotechnology could have a revolutionary impact. The cells that make up the human body are composed of nanoscale components. DNA, which is situated in the nucleus of a cell, is about two nanometers wide. Viruses are about fifty nanometers long. Bacteria and cells are huge by comparison, measuring in the thousands of nanometers. If scientists become proficient in manipulating matter at a nanoscale range, it would enable doctors to interact with the components of the human body at the subcellular level.

Diagnosis

Nanotechnology has the potential to improve patients' chances of recovery through early detection of medical conditions. An early diagnosis would give doctors a chance to battle cancer before it has spread throughout the body or treat a disease before it has caused irreversible damage.

Current technology cannot detect cancer cells, for example, until the tumor has grown to a significant size. The use of quantum dots could enable detection almost at the onset of the growth of cancerous cells. Scientists can affix specific molecules to quantum dots. For cancer research, they choose a molecule that will bind to a specific type of tumor cell. When injected into the bloodstream, the molecules attach themselves—and the quantum dots—to the cells of the tumor. The quantum dots are then charged with energy by illumination from a light source. The quantum dots produce a glow that can be scanned and photographed.

Different quantum dots emit different wavelengths of light. Conceivably, a patient could be injected with a solution containing several different types of quantum dots, each designed to adhere to a certain type of malignant cell. The doctor could then scan for various types of cancer with a single test. The different colors of light would signify the location and type of malignancies.

Quantum dots are just one type of nanoscale probe. Researchers are investigating many possible nanoparticle probes that will track conditions at a cellular and molecular level.

This is an artist's representation of quantum dot nanoparticles attaching themselves to a tumor on the wall of a blood vessel.

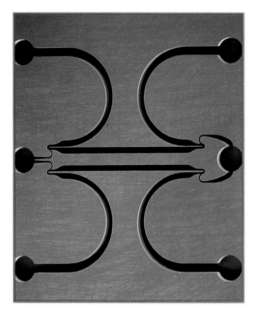

A microelectromechanical system (MEMS), such as this microfluidic chip, is a system or machine existing on the microscale. Other MEMS include sensors, switches, motors, and labs-on-a-chip.

Another potential breakthrough for diagnosis takes miniaturization to the nanoscale level. It is called "lab-on-a-chip" (LOC), or biochip. A single microchip moves a liquid sample through nanoscale channels and past sensors that would screen it for the presence of substances such as viruses or chemical agents. The lab-on-a-chip would be automated, portable, and nearly instantaneous. Chips called microarrays, and the further miniaturized nanoarrays, are already being used for DNA analysis.

Treatment and Repair

Nanotechnology will also provide advances in treating medical conditions once diagnosed. One of the most promising areas of research and development is in drug delivery technology. Conventional methods of delivering drugs, like pills, injections, and intravenous (IV) drips, do not allow precise control of the medicine's release.

Nanotechnology could provide the means of gradually releasing a drug into the body so that its concentration in the blood remained level throughout treatment and targeting a specific area for drug release.

This would be especially useful in administering chemotherapy, the treatment for cancer. Chemotherapy drugs kill cancer cells, but they also attack healthy cells, causing hair loss and other severe side effects. Targeted delivery would reduce side effects and allow higher dosages, since only cancer cells would be affected. Nanoshells, nanoscale glass beads coated with gold, could someday achieve this goal. Once injected into the bloodstream, nanoshells bind to tumors. The nanoshells would then be activated by an outside laser, causing them to emit heat and kill cancer cells.

A drug's rate of release over time can be controlled by nanoscale packaging of the drug molecules. The drug can be encapsulated inside a polymer, a large carbon-based molecule, which releases the drug gradually through pores. The size of the pores determines the rate of delivery. Two other molecules show great promise in drug delivery and potentially in gene therapy, the insertion of stretches of DNA and RNA into cells to replace damaged genes. Dendrimers, a type of large artificial molecule, have pockets within them ideal for carrying drug molecules. Structures called liposomes can bond to specific cells and release the drug.

Nanotechnology even holds promise for bioengineers working on the regeneration of entire organs in the laboratory. An artificial scaffolding would be populated with cells containing a patient's genetic material. The structure would grow into the desired organ, like a kidney or liver. The customized organ would have a low risk of rejection in the body, and the patient would not have to rely on a donor. Researchers have already developed materials based on nano-tubes that bond to bone, which provides an attachment for artificial joints or, potentially, a scaffolding for regeneration.

A technician uses an interference microscope (surface profiler) to examine a microelectromechanical system (MEMS). Its surface features are shown on the monitor.

Nanotechnology Careers in Health Care

Someday, hospitals will count nanotechnology experts among the specialists on their staff. Doctors, nurses, technicians, and other medical workers with nanotechnology expertise will be in high demand.

But the nanotechnology revolution in health care will occur slowly. Even for conventional drugs, it usually takes more than a decade for pharmaceutical companies to bring a product to market. After a drug is patented, the company must gain approval for clinical trials from the FDA. Only after multiple trials have confirmed its safety and effectiveness can it be approved for use. For nanotechnology products, which take a radically new approach to treating disease, the process will last even longer.

Still, there are exciting opportunities in the medical field for biologists, chemists, bioengineers, pharmacologists, research doctors, and other nanotechnology experts. Private companies, educational institutions, and various government departments are investing considerable funds and resources toward medical applications of nanotechnology. Nanotechnology experts will be needed to help shepherd medical products toward federal approval. Even though medical nanotechnology is still largely in its experimental stage, it is a realm of great potential for doctors and scientists who want to be among the pioneers in the field.

CHAPTER 4

Nanotechnology Jobs

As we've already seen, nanotechnology is a truly interdisciplinary pursuit. Chemists, biologists, physicists, and medical doctors all have a role in the field. Computer scientists join bioengineers, electrical engineers, chemical engineers, and mechanical engineers in working with matter at the nanoscale. Someday, there may be professional nanotechnologists, but today most nanotechnology experts specialize in the aspects of their own field.

Scientists

Scientists in a number of disciplines are conducting the exciting research that will eventually serve as a foundation for a nanotechnology revolution. In addition to research, scientists participate in every step of the process of bringing a nanotech product to market. Scientists must have a solid background in all of the basic branches of science, as well as specialized knowledge in their own discipline. Most positions require computer expertise, especially nanotech-related jobs. Scientific work requires analytical thinking, a high degree of accuracy and precision, and the ability to work well either individually or as part of a team. Scientific jobs involving nanotechnology generally require an advanced degree.

Physicists

Physicists study matter and energy and their interactions. Physics is sometimes called the "fundamental science," since the laws of physics underlie every other branch of science. Regardless of their particular discipline, physicists tend to focus on theoretical physics, experimental physics, or applied physics. Physicists in all three areas contribute to developments in nanotechnology. They earn a median salary of about $87,500.

Chemists

Chemists study the composition, structure, and properties of matter and the transformations matter undergoes during processes such as chemical reactions. Chemistry is a vast field, and most chemists work in a particular area. Chemists are at the forefront of academic research in nanotechnology. They're also employed in many of the industries pursuing nanotechnology, like the pharmaceutical and energy industries. Chemists earn a median salary of about $57,000.

Biologists

Biologists are the scientists who study living organisms and their vital processes. Biology is a huge field of science, with myriad branches of specialization that often overlap. Nanotechnology is an

Charles M. Lieber is a renowned Harvard University professor and founder of the nanotechnology company NanoSys, Inc. He is known for his pioneering work in the construction of nanowires.

area of interest in a number of different biological disciplines. Molecular biologists, for instance, study biology at the molecular level, which is also the nanoscale level. Biology and chemistry intersect in biochemistry, the study of the chemistry of living organisms. Biologists earn a median salary of about $51,000.

Materials Scientists

Materials scientists study the basic properties and functions of natural and man-made materials. Materials science is an interdisciplinary field that ranges across different branches of science and engineering. Although not a high-profile area of study, materials science is of vital importance to engineers working on projects from engines to skyscrapers. The emergence of a potential nanotechnology revolution has elicited a surge of interest in the possibilities of materials science, one of the areas of science most closely involved with nanotechnology. Materials scientists earn a median salary of about $70,500.

Pharmacologists

Pharmacologists study how drugs and other chemical substances interact with living organisms. They create drugs, test them, and analyze their effects. Nanotechnology has the potential to bring about a new generation of pharmaceuticals and drug delivery systems. Pharmacologists will oversee the creation of these new treatments, test their safety and effectiveness, recommend dosages, and determine appropriate circumstances for their use. In addition, they will study the general effects of nanoparticles of all kinds on humans and other organisms. Pharmacology requires a high degree of training and at least a doctorate degree. Pharmacologists are well compensated: Ph.D. pharmacologists entering the workplace earn an average salary of about $72,000 during their first few years of work.

Computer Scientists

Computer scientists conduct research into fundamental computer and information science. They work on both computer hardware and software. Computer scientists range from theorists employed by academic institutions to programmers, graphics designers, and network systems analysts. Computer science requires some formal education, at least a bachelor's degree, but relevant work experience is also highly desirable. These scientists are exploring how nanotechnology can be put to use in designing new computer drives, memory, and microchips. Computer scientists earn a median salary of about $88,000.

Engineers

Engineers apply scientific and mathematical knowledge to the design and construction of everyday products, machines, and structures. There are many branches of engineering, some of which can involve nanotechnology. Engineering generally requires a strong scientific background, problem-solving skills, analytical thinking, and close attention to details. In addition, most jobs in engineering involve teamwork and leadership opportunities. Engineers must complete at least a bachelor's degree, and some states require additional licensing or certification. Median salaries for engineers range from $67,000 to $81,000, depending on the particular discipline.

Mechanical Engineers

Mechanical engineering is the broadest field of engineering. Engineers in this field work with machinery and other such systems that convert energy into usable forms. They participate in every stage of a machine's production, from research and development to installation and maintenance. Specialized mechanical engineers are involved in nearly every aspect of nanotechnology, including the production of nano-materials, computing, energy, and robotics.

Electrical Engineers

Electrical engineers work with equipment that generates and distributes electric power. Electronics engineering, a subfield of electrical engineering, focuses on the electronic components of such devices as computers and telephones. Electrical engineers work on generators, transformers, and transmission lines, while electronics engineers work on integrated circuits and microprocessors. Microelectronics engineering concentrates on small-scale components, like transistors that make up computer chips. Nanotechnology could eventually make possible the development of smaller and more novel electronic components such as transistors made up of nanomaterials and light-generating nanoparticles for lightbulbs.

Chemical Engineers

Chemical engineers are involved with the conversion of raw materials into useful forms. They work on developing products such as fertilizers, detergents, plastics, gasoline, and foodstuffs, and oversee projects such as water treatment and mineral refinement. Unlike scientists in a lab, chemical engineers generally concentrate on the large-scale production of marketable products. They must take into account a number of factors in designing chemical facilities and production processes, like cost efficiency, environmental safety, and transport methods. One of the more versatile fields of engineering, chemical engineering is also utilized in nanotechnology. Chemical engineers work in the production of nanoparticles and the development of other nanomaterials.

Biomedical Engineers

Biomedical engineers—the term often used interchangeably with "bioengineers"—bring the principles of engineering to medicine and the life sciences. Biomedical engineers design medical diagnostic and monitoring equipment, as well as devices such as prosthetics and artificial organs. Some biomedical engineers modify genetic material, either to create living organisms with certain desirable traits or for potential use in a nonbiological context, like components of electronic devices. Nanotechnology, which has great potential in a number of medical applications, is a valuable tool in the exciting field of biomedical engineering.

Optical Engineers

Optics, which brings together physics and engineering, is the study of phenomena related to light. Engineers in this field apply the science

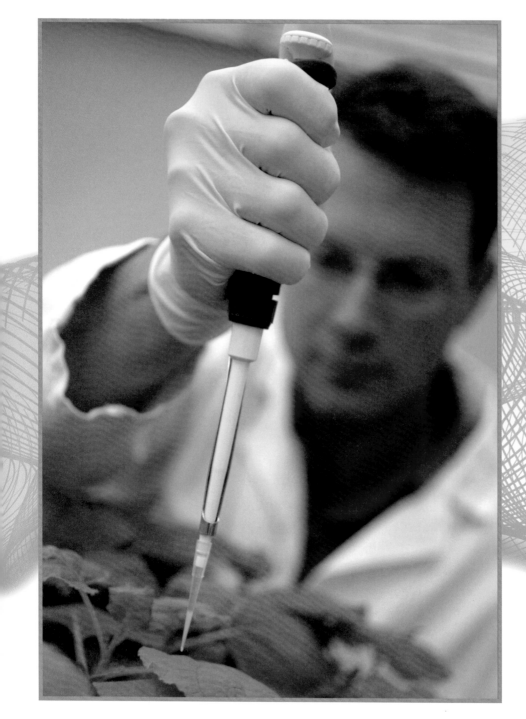

A biotech researcher "inoculates" a tobacco plant with a genetically engineered virus. Nanotechnology provides powerful tools and materials for understanding and manipulating biological systems.

of optics to the design of various kinds of equipment. They design instruments such as microscopes and telescopes, in addition to optical sensors, optical communications networks, and lasers. Optical engineers are exploring nanotechnology as a means of creating faster communications networks, as well as in other applications.

Software Engineers

Software engineers develop and customize computer software for particular industries or companies. Unlike other engineering disciplines, software engineering does not require an exceptionally strong scientific background. Software engineers designing software for nanotech research and development, however, should have a firm understanding of the concepts and potentials of nanotechnology. Nanotech labs and start-up companies generally require software to visualize matter at the nanoscale and create computer models in designing nanomaterials, pharmaceuticals, and other products.

Other Nanotech-Related Jobs

Medical researchers investigate diseases and other aspects of human health. Many of the specialists already profiled, like biologists, pharmacologists, and biomedical engineers, may conduct medical research. But in order to work with patients, a medical researcher must also be a licensed physician. Scientists who have earned both a Ph.D. and a medical degree have a significant advantage in performing research. Nurses who have completed a master's degree or higher may also specialize in research. Before nanotechnology treatments and medical products reach the market, medical researchers will have to take them through exhaustive testing and clinical trials.

Technicians assist scientists, engineers, and medical researchers in their work. Although working in lower-level positions, technicians involved in nanotechnology still require a high degree of skill and

Designers and software engineers work in their cubicles at a division of Sony Computer Entertainment in Tokyo, Japan.

training. Microfabrication technicians, for example, specialize in the processes used in creating products such as microchips. Electrical engineering technicians help design and test equipment. Medical technicians perform lab analyses of blood and other samples.

Science writers present scientific information in a variety of different forms. These range from formal reports published in scientific journals to news accounts of new discoveries. Books and articles may be intended for a limited readership of experts in a particular field or for the general public. Science writers must possess excellent writing and research skills, as well as a keen interest in their subject. It is important that science writers remain objective, especially when covering topics such as nanotechnology that receive a large amount of media attention. Positions may require a college degree in communications, journalism, or English, and a strong background in science. Writers earn a median salary of about $45,000, although earnings vary greatly depending on the position.

CHAPTER 5

Cutting Edge Careers
Cutting Edge Careers
Careers
Cutting Edge Careers

In Development

Within a few years, nanotech products related to information technology and health care will be commercially available. As manufacturers begin to take advantage of the improvements made possible by nanomaterials, they will release more and more products incorporating nanoparticles and utilizing other applications of nanotechnology.

In other industries, it will take longer for nanotechnology to realize its potential. The transportation industry, for example, could benefit hugely from nanotechnology. Nanolubricants and coatings could keep vehicles running more smoothly and prevent breakdowns. The usage of strong, lightweight nanotubes in manufacturing could greatly reduce a car's weight. Nanotechnology could help the auto and aerospace industries achieve better fuel efficiency and reduced emissions. But if manu-facturers do embrace nanotechnology, these improvements will be slow in coming. It is hard to predict when nanotechnology will bring innovation to the transportation industry, and even harder to envision how this will affect the future job market in the industry.

Likewise, nanotechnology has the potential to bring dramatic change and job growth to other fields, but it is difficult to guess if and when this will occur. Three such areas are energy and the environment, the military, and space exploration.

Energy and the Environment

Today, the need for energy is critical. As the world population grows and more countries become industrialized, energy requirements will increase. Meanwhile, the United States relies heavily on fossil fuels, a diminishing resource. Nanotechnology could transform the outlook on energy by making possible more efficient usage of existing resources, while advancing alternative energy sources such as solar and fuel cells.

Oil must be processed and refined into a usable product. This is done through chemical reactions accelerated by compounds called catalysts. The use of nanoparticles as catalysts could improve the effectiveness of the reaction and reduce the amount of energy necessary to perform the reaction. A nanocatalyst can, for example, improve the process of refining oil into gasoline. Even more radical is the use of nanocatalysts in turning coal into liquid fuel. They could also be used in the industrial production of chemicals, making the process more energy efficient and environmentally friendly.

Nanotechnology could help reduce energy consumption in our daily lives. Currently under development by a number of companies, batteries improved by nanotechnology would be smaller, cheaper, and more powerful. Rechargeable batteries, especially lithium-ion

Nanotechnology holds great promise for automobiles of the future. This Mitsubishi concept car is powered by lithium ion batteries. Nanotech devices and materials could also improve the function and durability of automobiles.

batteries, would hold their charge longer and take less time to recharge. Lightbulbs incorporating quantum dots would save energy by converting electricity into light with very little power wasted. In conventional lightbulbs, about 90 percent of their electricity usage is lost through generation of heat.

However, nanotechnology's greatest promise in the energy industry is in alternative energy sources. Solar cells are presently too expensive for most companies or individuals to utilize on a large scale. They are costly to manufacture and install. Current manufacturing techniques require expensive equipment and manipulation of the solar cell at high temperatures. The solar cell of the future will likely be made of plastic embedded with nanoparticles. Experimental nanotech solar cells can be printed out in sheets by an ink-jet printer. Someday, solar cells may be made from fabric or encased in the glass of windowpanes.

Hydrogen fuel cells could provide a pollution-free source of energy. These have the potential to fuel cars or generate power in a building. Functional fuel cells have already been developed and even used in spacecraft, but the disadvantages of bringing the technology down to Earth lie in handling the fuel, hydrogen gas. Nanotechnology might someday contribute to energy-efficient hydrogen gas production and compact storage.

These applications indirectly benefit the environment through energy conservation, but nanotechnology also has the potential to help clean up our air and water. In factories, air filters studded with nanocrystals could reduce emissions of pollutants such as carbon dioxide and mercury. Similarly, water filters made of carbon nanotubes or nanofibers could purify water of viruses and microbes, providing safe drinking water in areas with a short supply of it. On a larger scale, nanoparticles could be pumped into contaminated water sources, where they would neutralize harmful chemicals.

Warfare

Many applications of nanotechnology have military potential. Military spending makes up almost a third of the funds being allocated by the U.S. National Nanotechnology Initiative. Every branch of the military is involved in nanotechnology programs.

One of the military's most high-profile programs is the Institute for Soldier Nanotechnology (ISN), launched by MIT under a contract with the army. The ISN's main focus is the development of a battle suit intended to reduce casualty rates in conflict. The suit will take advantage of many of the unique properties of nanomaterials, as well as the miniaturization made possible by nanotechnology. The suit will be lightweight and bulletproof, and the material itself will have the

Soldiers model two uniform systems under development. The Vision 2020 Future Warrior concept *(left)* will incorporate sensors, robotics systems, durable armor, and other improvements made possible by nanotechnology.

ability to treat injuries. It will contain an automatic communication system. Sensors embedded in the material will detect and protect against the presence of chemical and biological agents in the area. Possibly, it will have "exomuscles" that augment the soldier's own strength.

The military partners with a number of companies that do not specialize in military applications of nanotechnology but whose products might be useful in a military context. Water filtration systems could be invaluable to soldiers on the field. Nanostructured steel and other composites could strengthen military equipment, buildings, and bridges. Sensors incorporating nanoparticles could detect traces of chemical or biological agents, and other nanomaterials might detoxify these agents. Similarly, lab-on-a-chip technology could provide quick, on-the-spot analysis of unknown substances.

Nanotechnology could also be used to improve weapons. Firearms could be developed that do not contain any metal. Improved munitions would be more powerful and better controlled.

Taking Nanotechnology into Outer Space

Nanotechnology's promise in a wide range of fields—health, energy, computing, materials science, electronics, and more—could be used to revolutionize space exploration. NASA is constantly investigating technologies with potential applications in spacecraft and related equipment. One ongoing project is the development of lighter, stronger, more durable materials. Carbon nanotubes, with their light weight and great strength, could have many uses, from structural composites to wiring.

Miniaturization made possible by nanotechnology will lead to smaller, more powerful instruments. Nanosensors could monitor equipment for any malfunctions, and nanotechnology could be used for the creation of self-repairing materials. Miniature spacecraft could be deployed and controlled from a shuttle or space station, reducing the need for astronauts to undertake space walks for routine observations. For unmanned missions, nanotechnology could be used in probes and rovers designed for planetary exploration.

Applications of nanotechnology could greatly improve the safety of space exploration. Nanomaterials would make space suits safer and more functional. The lab-on-a-chip and other medical advances would allow the diagnosis and treatment of health problems in space. Advanced fuel cells and solar cells could be used for energy requirements, even as nanotechnology made equipment more energy-efficient. This would be of vital importance on longer manned missions, like a trip to Mars.

Nanotechnology may someday bring about a dream long held by space enthusiasts: an elevator that could provide a new means of putting people and goods into space. A tower located on the equator would tether a cable structure—the tracks for the elevator—to Earth. The elevator would be connected to a satellite in geostationary orbit, meaning it would always remain directly above the same location on Earth. Nanomaterials such as carbon nanotubes would be used in the cables and other structural components.

Nanotechnology and the Distant Future

Many writers have indulged themselves in speculation about the ultimate future of nanotechnology. Most agree that nanotechnology will eventually lead to a revolution in medicine, although they paint different hypothetical scenarios. "Smart" chips implanted in our bodies will detect medical conditions and synthesize treatments. Nanoscale implants will reverse loss of sight and hearing. Molecular medicines will treat Alzheimer's and other diseases. Cars will be piloted by computers. Television and computer screens will be rendered obsolete as more people have images transmitted directly to implants

An artist's rendering shows a space elevator extending from the equator to a space station. Such an elevator, constructed of nanomaterials, could someday reduce the risk and expense of space travel.

on the retinas of their eyes. People will be able to choose between DNA computers that store and manipulate information with DNA molecules, or powerful quantum computers that use the principles of quantum mechanics. The list goes on.

Some of these innovations may arrive sooner than one might expect, while others may never materialize. But futuristic speculation about the applications of nanotechnology is a long tradition in the field. In 1986, K. Eric Drexler published *Engines of Creation: The Coming Era of Nanotechnology*. In this book, he describes a hypothetical future of the world that inspired most nanotech scenarios in science fiction books such as Michael Crichton's *Prey*. Drexler imagined an "assembler" that could construct any object, atom by atom, through bottom-up fabrication. He also described a possible doomsday in which the world is taken over by "gray goo" made up of self-replicating nanoscale robots gone out of control.

Despite the sensationalistic aspects, the concepts introduced in *Engines of Creation* captured the imagination of many scientists. Molecular engineering became a top goal of some researchers. Among Drexler's early fans was Richard Smalley. But over the years, Smalley and others began to doubt the possibility of molecular assembly as outlined in Drexler's book. In 2003, there was no mention of molecular manufacturing in the 21st Century Nanotechnology Research and Development Act.

A small group of nanotechnology proponents still subscribes to Drexler's vision. They consider the contemporary usage of the term "nanotechnology" a diluted version of the field's original ambitions. Instead, they advocate an alternative term, molecular nanotechnology (MNT), and hold faith in the feasibility of molecular manufacturing, complete with molecular machines and assembly lines for the construction of molecular structures.

Most nanotechnology experts doubt that such molecular manufacturing will ever come to pass. Still, MNT supporters illustrate the broad potential of nanotechnology. There is room for visionaries, as well as scientists, engineers, computer scientists, and medical researchers. Nanotechnology will bring about everyday improvements in our clothes and vehicles, and the major transformations of entire industries. Some nanotech start-ups will become household names, and some large corporations will find a new focus in the field. Nanotechnology professionals will pursue a variety of promising career paths across the many related fields. Nanotechnology holds an exciting range of potential.

GLOSSARY

buckminsterfullerene A spherical nanoparticle consisting of sixty carbon atoms. It was named in honor of R. Buckminster Fuller, the visionary and architect remembered particularly for his development of the geodesic dome. A buckminsterfullerene resembles a geodesic dome.

catalyst A substance that initiates or accelerates a chemical reaction without being consumed in the process.

chemotherapy The treatment of cancer through chemicals that are selectively toxic to malignant cells and tissues.

DNA (deoxyribonucleic acid) The nucleic acid found in the nucleus of the cell that carries the genetic information and hereditary characteristics.

fabrication The manufacture of something from raw materials.

malignant Tending to invade and destroy nearby tissue and potentially spreading to other parts of the body (used to describe a tumor).

molecule The smallest particle of a substance (an element or compound) that retains the chemical properties of the substance; two or more atoms held together by chemical bonds.

munitions Military supplies, especially weapons and ammunition.

nano One-billionth, from the Greek word for "dwarf."

polymer A compound, usually carbon-based, consisting of large molecules made by the linking together of smaller molecules called monomers.

quantum mechanics The branch of physics that describes the behavior of objects at the atomic level.

semiconductor A material that has a conductivity greater than that of an insulator but less than that of a conductor.

silicon A nonmetallic element that is abundant in the earth's crust.

subcellular On a smaller level of size than a cell.

tensile strength The maximum amount of tension a material can withstand without tearing apart.

transistor An electronic semiconductor device with at least three electrical contacts that is used in a circuit as a switch, amplifier, or detector.

FOR MORE
INFORMATION

ASME Nanotechnology Institute
3 Park Avenue
New York, NY 10016
(212) 591-7789
Web site: http://www.nanotechnologyinstitute.org

Institute for Soldier Nanotechnologies
Massachusetts Institute of Technology
Building NE47, 4th Floor
77 Massachusetts Avenue
Cambridge, MA 02139
(617) 324-4700
Web site: http://web.mit.edu/isn

International Association of Nanotechnology
2386 Fair Oaks Boulevard
Sacramento, CA 95825
(916) 529-4119 or (916) 481-8100
Web site: http://www.ianano.org

Nano Science and Technology Institute
One Kendall Square, PMB 308
Cambridge, MA 02139
(508) 357-2925
Web site: http://www.nsti.org

National Nanotechnology Initiative
4201 Wilson Boulevard
Stafford II, Room 405
Arlington, VA 22230
(703) 292-4399
Web site: http://www.nano.gov

Small Times
Small Times Media, LLC
655 Phoenix Drive
Ann Arbor, MI 48108
(734) 994-1106
Web site: http://www.smalltimes.com

Web Sites

Due to the changing nature of Internet links, Rosen Publishing has developed an online list of Web sites related to the subject of this book. This site is updated regularly. Please use this link to access the list:

http://www.rosenlinks.com/cec/nano

FOR FURTHER READING

Bridgman, Roger. *Eyewitness: Technology*. New York, NY: DK Eyewitness Books, 2000.

Darling, David. *Beyond 2000: Micromachines and Nanotechnology: The Amazing New World of the Ultrasmall*. New York, NY: Dillon Press, 1995.

Johnson, Rebeccah L. *Nanotechnology* (Cool Science). Minneapolis, MN: Lerner Publications, 2005.

Maddox, Diane. *Nanotechnology* (Science on the Edge). San Diego, CA: Blackbirch Press, 2005.

Shell, Barry. *Sensational Scientists: The Journeys and Discoveries of 24 Men and Women of Science*. Vancouver, BC: Raincoast Books, 2006.

BIBLIOGRAPHY

Atkinson, William Illsey. *Nanocosm: Nanotechnology and the Big Changes Coming from the Inconceivably Small*. New York, NY: Amacom, 2005.

Booker, Richard, and Earl Boysen. *Nanotechnology for Dummies*. Hoboken, NJ: Wiley Publishing, Inc., 2005.

Hall, J. Storrs. *Nanofuture: What's Next for Nanotechnology*. Amherst, NY: Prometheus Books, 2005.

Price, Steven. "Audacious & Outrageous: Space Elevators." NASA Science News, September 7, 2000. Retrieved April 2006 (http://science.nasa.gov/headlines/y2000/ast07sep_1.htm).

Sargent, Ted. *The Dance of Molecules: How Nanotechnology Is Changing Our Lives*. New York, NY: Thunder's Mouth Press, 2006.

Scientific American, Inc. *Understanding Nanotechnology*. New York, NY: Time Warner Book Group, 2002.

Uldrich, Jack. *Investing in Nanotechnology: Think Small, Win Big*. Avon, MA: Platinum Press, 2006.

Uldrich, Jack, with Deb Newberry. *The Next Big Thing Is Really Small: How Nanotechnology Will Change the Future of Your Business*. New York, NY: Crown Business, 2003.

Wolfe, Josh. "Top Nano Products of 2005." *Forbes*/Wolfe Nanotech Report, January 16, 2006. Retrieved April 2006 (http://www.forbes.com/technology/2006/01/10/apple-nano-in_jw_0109soapbox.inl.html).

INDEX

About the Author

Corona Brezina is a writer and researcher who lives in Chicago, Illinois. She has written many young adult titles, the subjects of which range from history and country profiles to science. She is excited at the prospect of being witness to the nanotech revolution.

Photo Credits

Cover (top) © Department of Energy Photo; cover (bottom), p. 38 © Voler Steger/Photo Researchers, Inc.; pp. 4–5 Bruce Rolff/Shutterstock.com; p. 5 © Harvey of Pasadena/AIP/Photo Researchers, Inc.; p. 6 © Stephen Jaffe/AFP/Getty Images; p. 8 © Paul Sakuma/AP/Wide World Photos; p. 11 © Tim Thompson/The Oakland Press/AP/Wide World Photos; pp. 13, 16 © Michael Conroy/AP/Wide World Photos; p. 18 © Mike Derer/AP/Wide World Photos; p. 21 © Kenneth EwardBioGrafx/Photo Researchers, Inc.; pp. 22, 34 © Colin Cuthbert/Photo Researchers, Inc.; p. 25 © David Paul Morris/Getty Images; p. 31 © Kenneth Eward/Photo Researchers, Inc.; p. 32 © David Scharf/Photo Researchers, Inc.; p. 42 © Michael Maloney/San Francisco Chronicle/Corbis; p. 44 © Tom Wagner/Corbis Saba; p. 48 © Toru Yamanaka/AFP/Getty Images; p. 50 photo by Phil Copeland/United States Department of Defense; p. 53 Handout/epa/Corbis.

Editor: Wayne Anderson; Series Designer: Evelyn Horovicz
Photo Researcher: Hilary Arnold